More

Dark Man

Danger in the Dark
by Peter Lancett
illustrated by Jan Pedroietta

Published by Ransom Publishing Ltd.
51 Southgate Street, Winchester, Hampshire SO23 9EH
www.ransom.co.uk

ISBN   978 184167 415 5

First published in 2006
Second printing 2008

Printed in China through Colorcraft Ltd., Hong Kong.

Dark Man

Danger in the Dark

by Peter Lancett

illustrated by Jan Pedroietta

Ransom

Chapter One:
The Girl

The Dark Man is not alone.

The girl is with him.

They are walking in the bad part of the city at night.

The Dark Man has found her.

He must take her to the Old Man.

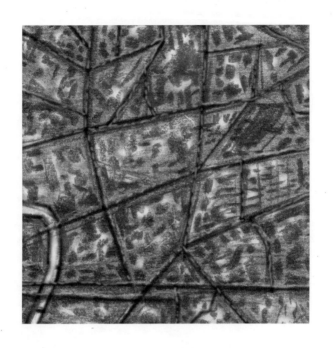

The Old Man is in a safe place.

Chapter Two:
Demons on the Streets

The girl is very scared.

The Shadow Masters want to find her.

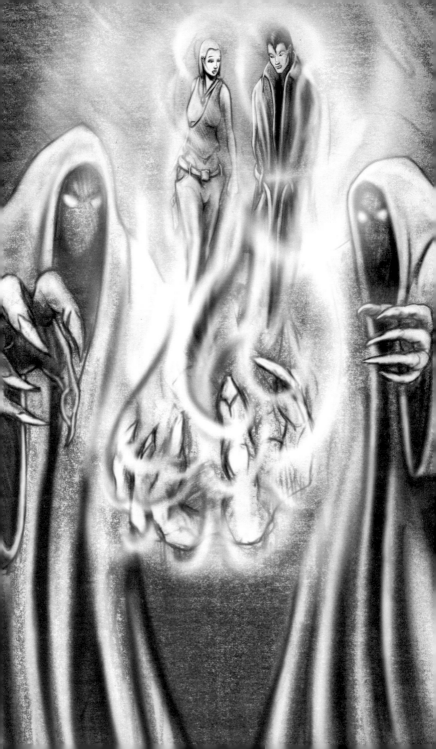

She has a secret power.

The Shadow Masters will use her to find a magic stone.

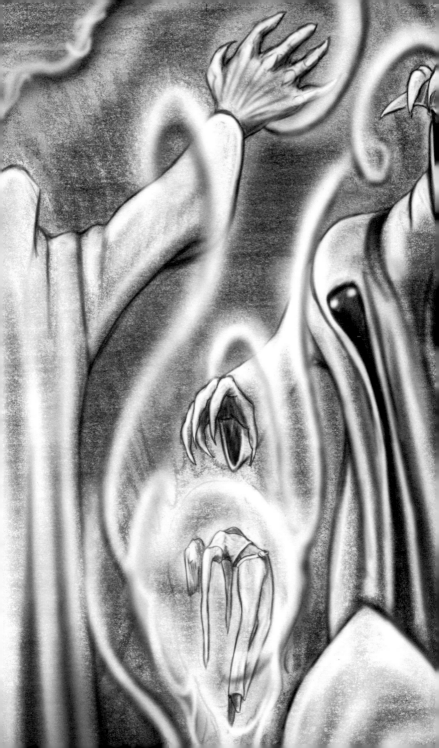

Because it is night, they have put demons on the streets.

The demons can look like men.

Chapter Three:
The Dog

A dog comes around a corner.

The Dark Man stops and the girl hides behind him.

She holds his coat.

The dog could be a demon.

Demons have come in the shape of animals before.

This dog just walks across the road.

Chapter Four:
Danger in the Dark

The Dark Man and the girl walk on.

Now they can see the lights in the good part of the city.

Soon they will be at the place where the Old Man waits.

The Dark Man cannot feel safe.

The streets here are still dark.

There are shadows all around.

There are dark doorways where demons can hide.

Soon they will be safe, but the Dark Man does not rest.

It is dark.

There is always danger in the dark.

The author

photograph: Rachel Ottewill

Peter Lancett used to work in the movies. Then he worked in the city. Now he writes horror stories for a living. "It beats having a proper job," he says.